**FRIENDS
OF ACPL**

W9-CVA-654

The Repair of Uncle Toe

THE REPAIR
OF UNCLE TOE

Story and Pictures by Kay Chorao

Farrar, Straus and Giroux

N E W   Y O R K

Library of Congress catalog card number: 77-184129

ISBN 0-374-36245-9

First printing, 1972

Published simultaneously in Canada by

Doubleday Canada, Ltd., Toronto

Printed in the United States of America

Designed by Cynthia Krupat

The Repair of Uncle Toe

Sam had always lived with his grandmother, but
now she was growing too ill to look after him. So it was
decided that Sam should live with his Uncle Toe.

When it was time, the lady who nursed Grandma
put Sam on the train.

"Don't worry, Sammy," she said. "Grandma will bring
you back when she is feeling better."

But Sam wasn't sure that Grandma would ever feel
better. He sat in the train all day long, looking out at the
sky. Once, a cloud shaped like a whale seemed to open
its mouth and yawn.

A lady from Travelers Aid met Sam at the train station and drove him to Uncle Toe's house, which was also a shop where Uncle Toe repaired shoes.

"Hello, I'm Sam," said Sam.

"Yes, yes, well, come in," said Uncle Toe.

Sam hoped that Uncle Toe would read to him the way
Grandma had. But Uncle Toe didn't have time to read,
or to make up stories, or to play with Sam the way his
grandmother had.

Before, Sam had been allowed to do what he pleased.

Now, Uncle Toe roared at him to chew his food properly,

and to tidy his room, and to hitch up his socks.

"Please read to me, Uncle," begged Sam, trying to match his uncle's giant steps.

"I can't lallygag and waste time now that I have another mouth to feed," boomed Uncle Toe.

Then the old man stormed into his shop, where he cut leather into shoe shapes, pounded new heels onto worn-out ones, and made the ceiling shake with the noise of his stitching machine.

Sam listened to the rumble in his room above the shop. He wished that the pounding and stitching would stop, that Uncle Toe would come and play.

But Uncle Toe never came.

So Sam played with Brute, a dog Grandma had made
out of an old blanket when Sam was two.

Brute was sometimes called Captain Eagle and he had
real fur ears made from Grandma's old Persian lamb muff.

Sometimes Brute stole a peek at himself in the mirror.

He was especially proud of his Captain Eagle cape.

Sam hugged his friend and covered him with stars for being so good.

But one day Uncle Toe found Sam playing with Brute.

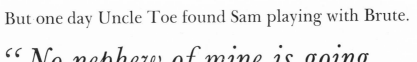

"No nephew of mine is going to waste time with dolls," he bellowed.

"Put that silly thing away and sweep the floor! This room is a disgraceful *mess!*" roared Uncle Toe.

Sam hugged Captain Eagle. "NO!" he cried.

So Uncle Toe grabbed poor Brute, he gave him a fearful toss, and thundered away.

"Children, hummmmmmmmmmph," he muttered.

The more Uncle Toe thought about Sam, the madder
he became.

"All they think about is fun and wasting time!"

"Thankless child can only muddle things up and
lallygag with a dirty rag doll."

Uncle Toe set to work and in his anger he hit his finger
with a hammer.

"*Rats!*" he shouted. He was filled with such rage that his heart, which had always been leathery at the edges, grew as hard as an old boot.

And as Uncle Toe stomped and jigged and roared and yelled, the leather grew and grew and grew until Uncle Toe was one enormous *shoe!*

"Fiddle, boy, don't just stand there. *Do* something," cried Uncle Toe.

"But, Uncle, you look just like a shhhhhh—"

"NONSENSE," interrupted Uncle Toe. "Help me up. Give me a push! Rub my joints with oil! Find some saddle soap! HELP ME, BOY!"

"NO!"

And Sam ran away to find Captain Eagle, who was looking quite glum and pale, wedged between some spats and a bottle of hair-grow on Uncle Toe's bureau.

Now Sam could do as he pleased.

He could jump and somersault on the beds with his shoes on.

He could play with water and run it as hard as he liked.
He could lean out the window and even crawl out on
Uncle Toe's boot sign so that everyone in town might see
him and whisper, "My, what a brave wild boy that Sam is."

At last Sam got tired of sliding down the banister.

"I'm hungry," he thought to himself.

While Sam had played, the sun had slipped behind the buildings, leaving a dark city filled with shadows and strange blinking lights, like eyes. Somewhere a clothesline squeaked, a cat howled, and a siren screamed. To Sam they were the voices of ugly things with claws and scales. He could see things move and blink at him through the kitchen window.

The stove was usually warm and friendly, but now it was cold and it seemed to watch Sam with secret eyes.

Sam wasn't hungry after all. He was scared.

Hugging Captain Eagle, Sam ran as fast as he could from the kitchen, down the dark hall to his uncle's workshop.

"A fine kettle of fish," grunted Uncle Toe.

Sam rubbed his uncle's joints with saddle soap. He even mixed some lemon oil and hot water and rubbed the mixture all over his uncle's leathery hide.

Then Sam pushed and pushed and pushed his uncle, but it was of no use. A shoe the size of Cecil Toe could not be budged.

"This is no joke," grumbled Uncle Toe, squinting sideways at the length of his shoe-self.

"I'm hungry, Uncle," said Sam. "If you would change back the way you were before, I would sweep the floors for you, or polish shoes for customers, or *anything* you asked."

"Ha," said Uncle Toe slyly. "Would you throw away that dog?"

"His name is Captain Eagle," said Sam. "And no, I won't throw him away."

But when Sam ran back into the hallway he felt the blackness swallow him up. He felt all around him the eyes and scales and claws and blinking monster things of the night.

Hugging his dog for the last time, he ran to the window. Without stopping to think, for had he thought he never would have done such a thing, he threw Brute out.

Uncle Toe's heart was touched. Slowly, slowly it warmed. The warmth grew and bit by bit it became quite human.

"I really didn't think he would. Bless my soul," he whispered.

His eyes filled with warm salt tears and his shoe body shrank and shrank away.

Wobbling to his feet, Uncle Toe clapped his hands and laughed for joy. And when his strength returned, he clicked his heels and danced a circle around his hat.

TOE REP

Of course the first thing Uncle Toe did was to find Brute, who was disgruntled but otherwise fine.

And after that, and forever after, the nights were filled with stars instead of eyes or claws, and Uncle Toe read to Sam so often that even Uncle Toe knew all the words of Sam's books by heart.